CHRISTMAS HEARTS

NINA LEVINE

DEDICATION

For all my fierce Stormgirls.
Merry fucking Christmas!

CHRISTMAS HEARTS

Celebrate Christmas Stormgirl style.

Catch up with Winter & Birdie, Fury & Zara, King & Lily, and the rest of the Sydney Storm couples as they all come together to celebrate Christmas.

Expect your usual Storm level of sexy combined with the crazy antics of these Stormgirls.

And no Storm book would be complete without a bossy Storm man. King and Lily at Christmas? Expect some fireworks!

Come home for Christmas and find out what everyone has been up to in this Storm MC novella.

This is book three in the Storm MC Reloaded series and should be read in order.

Sign up for my newsletter to find out about new books, sales, and receive free bonus content.

If you're on Facebook, I have a reader group you can join to chat about my books with me, enter exclusive giveaways and read sneak peeks of upcoming books.

****

Storm MC Series

1. Storm
2. Fierce
3. Blaze
4. Revive
5. Slay
5.5 Sassy Christmas
6. Illusive
7. Command
8. Havoc

Sydney Storm MC Series

1. Relent

2. Nitro's Torment

3. Devil's Vengeance

4. Hyde's Absolution

5. King's Wrath

6. King's Reign

7. King: The Epilogue Collection

Storm MC Reloaded Series

1. Hurricane Hearts

2. War of Hearts

3. Christmas Hearts

4. Battle Hearts

Standalones:

Ashton Scott (bossy billionaire romance)

Steal My Breath (friends-to-lovers romance)

Be The One (rockstar romance)

Follow me on BookBub to hear about my sales

STORM MC TIMELINE

Hi guys!

I want to reacquaint you with the timeline of the Storm MC Reloaded series so that you can picture the events of this book.

HURRICANE HEARTS: Winter & Birdie get back together at the time of the events happening in King's Wrath/King's Reign.

FAST FORWARD 4 YEARS

WAR OF HEARTS:

Part 1 of that story, when Fury & Zara meet, happens a few months after the epilogue in King's

Reign, so this is FOUR YEARS AFTER King & Lily marry. Also four years after Winter & Birdie marry.

FAST FORWARD 4 YEARS

Part 2 of that story happens FOUR YEARS AFTER part 1.

CHRISTMAS HEARTS: happens four months after the end of War of Hearts. So at this point, both King & Lily, and Winter & Birdie have been married 8 years.

I hope this helps!

Nina x

PS clearly I like the number 4 ;)

1

Lily

"Cade King, if you don't come here right now, I'm texting Santa to let him know he shouldn't bring you a present this year!"

Zara rests her elbows on the kitchen counter between us and arches her brows at me. "Your stress levels have at least doubled since I saw you yesterday, Mum. What's going on?"

I widen my eyes in exasperation. Not at Zara, because she's the only one in my family not contributing to my stress, but rather at life in general. "My list is long. You really want me to detail it for you?"

She grins. "Your list is always long. King makes sure of that."

I throw the tea towel onto the counter and reach for the glass of cold water she poured me a minute ago. After I guzzle half, I take a deep breath and say, "It's this damn heat. And the kids. And the fact I'm nowhere near ready for our family dinner tonight or the barbecue tomorrow. And that I still don't know exactly how many are coming tomorrow afternoon, which makes catering for it hard. And that I still need to get the new swing set picked up. And well"—I widen my eyes some more—"at this point, I'm not even sure it'll get built in time for tomorrow." I rake my fingers through my hair, pushing it off my forehead where it's sticking from the bloody heat. "And don't even get me started on King. That man is testing me right now, and when he gets home, if he *ever* gets home, I have so many words for him that he won't know what hit him."

Zara's grin disappears and concern fills her features. "Okay, let's start at the beginning. The heat. Why haven't you gotten the air conditioning fixed in here? It's been out for two days and it's nearly forty degrees, which is—"

"King told me he'd be home yesterday and that he'd fix it, but now that he can't give me a confirmed ETA, I've called the air conditioning guy that Kree recommended." I throw my hands up in the air. "The only problem is, everyone and their dog in Sydney is having issues with their air conditioning, so God knows when he'll make it here."

She pulls out her phone and starts tapping away on it. "I'll get Fury to come take a look today." When she finishes texting, she meets my gaze again. "He's close by so he's coming now. I also asked him if he'd pick up your swing set, and we'll stay after dinner tonight and put it together for you if King isn't home by then. Now, as for tomorrow, if you give me a list of who hasn't RSVP'd yet, I'll ring around and find out so you can sort out the food you need."

I stare at my daughter. I swear she didn't come from me; nothing seems to ruffle her in the way it does me. "Whatever superpower pills you're on, I need some."

"Yeah, a chill pill wouldn't go astray, but I get it; this heat is enough to send anyone crazy and on top of that, you've got King doing a good job of it already."

I look around the kitchen wondering why my son isn't here yet. "Not to mention these kids! The heat is bringing out their worst behaviour. And your brother is about to learn that Santa isn't coming to him this year."

Zara reaches for me as I turn to leave the kitchen in search of Cade. "Let me go find him. And calm down about Santa. We both know there's no way you're really going to punish him in that way so don't make threats you won't keep." As she's exiting the room, she throws over her shoulder, "Make that list of who you need me to call. And then maybe guzzle some wine."

Wine at 10:00 a.m.?

Maybe a little early.

Maybe freaking not.

Not when King hasn't called for over twelve hours or replied to my calls or texts. Not when I have no idea when he'll be home from Melbourne or if he'll even make it in time for Christmas.

That bloody man.

A knock on my front door cuts through my thoughts. "Lil, can you help me? I've got meat for you," Tatum calls out.

I meet her at the door and take trays of steak and sausages from her. "Why are you bringing me meat?" We're holding a Christmas Day barbecue here tomorrow afternoon for the club, and King is covering the cost of all the food. He's also supposed to be collecting the meat from the butcher this afternoon, but I'm not even thinking about that right now because it may send my blood pressure through the roof.

"Nitro picked it up from the butcher for King this morning and asked me to bring it over."

I stare at her, willing my frustration with my

husband to maintain the level it's currently at rather than increasing a few levels. "It's so nice of King to call Nitro but not return any of his wife's calls."

"Your sarcasm is noted," she says, "but let's just get this meat inside before I die in this heat out here."

"Oh, you're gonna die in here too," Zara says, joining us. "But don't get Mum started on why the air con isn't fixed yet."

We carry all the meat into the kitchen and load it into the fridge, which is now almost full, when Fury enters the kitchen. He reaches for Zara and kisses her before turning his attention to me. "I'll check out the air con, but I'm no expert so I can't guarantee anything."

I silently thank the universe for my son-in-law-to-be and say, "Thank you. You're getting an extra present tomorrow for this."

Amusement crosses his face, but he doesn't respond to what I've said. He simply nods and exits the kitchen, meeting Cade on the way out.

My son has been giving me hell for weeks. Between arguing with me over every little thing, arguing with his brother and sister, and developing some bad behaviour that we've never seen from him before, I'm at my wits' end trying to figure out how to deal with him. I suspect it's because he's missing his father, but regardless of the why, I need to get a handle on this situation and I need to do that faster than I have been.

"Have you cleaned up that mess in your bedroom?" I ask. The mess I asked him to clean up last night. The mess he freaking added to instead of doing what I asked.

The defiance he stares back at me with does not make me want to give him the presents King and I bought him for Christmas. It's this defiance that his father is going to have to spend some time working on because I sure don't seem to be making any headway on it. "I'm nearly finished."

Cade's idea of nearly finished is vastly different to mine. "Right, you go back to your room and you stay there until it's done, and just so you know, Cade, Santa isn't fussed on visiting kids with messy rooms, so if you want him to visit you, I'd suggest getting your room as tidy as you can."

"That's not true! My room wasn't tidy last year."

I lift my brows, challenging him to continue down this path of arguing with me. "He also doesn't love it when children argue with their parents."

His mouth pinches together. "You're making this up! You don't know Santa! I don't have to clean my room!"

One.

Two.

Three.

I take a deep breath.

I love my son.

I love my son.

I love my son.

"You're right. I don't. Maybe you should try it your way and see if any of this is true. You'll know tomorrow morning when you either have presents from him or you don't."

Cade has the same eyes as his father. The brown in them darkens when he's experiencing a storm of emotions, and my words have triggered that storm inside him. Without another word, he turns and stalks out of the kitchen.

I take another deep breath and look at Zara. "Tell me you're staying here all day. I'm not sure I should be in charge of keeping Cade alive today."

"I'm here all day, and if I have to go out to get anything, I'll take him with me."

"You are the best daughter in the world."

She grins. "I'm telling Holly you said that."

My phone sounds with a text and my attention shifts completely to that, hoping it's from my husband. Praying it says something like "home in an hour."

KING: **Got bike problems. Should be home by dinner.**

Me: Should as in will?
King: Should.

I CALL him but he doesn't answer.
Oh my God, I will freaking kill him.

ME: **Answer your phone.**

HIS REPLY ISN'T instant but it does come.

KING: **I'm in the middle of sorting out some shit.**
    Me: **Well if you don't answer your phone or call
me, you're gonna be sorting out a whole heap of
shit you don't wanna be sorting out.**

A COUPLE OF MINUTES PASS, in which my chest
tightens with annoyance, frustration, and the
exhaustion I'm feeling from the kids. From the heat.
From life.
    And then his call comes through.
    I answer it like my life is ending and he's my life-
line. "I love you, King, but seriously you're testing

that love and if you don't make it home before dinner I may—"

"What's going on there?"

"Are you serious right now? *What's going on*? If you want a list, I'll be happy to give it to you, but you'll need longer than a couple of minutes to hear it. Maybe you'd like me to text it to you. I know you're not about phone calls this week." The high-pitched tone that has taken over my voice is one I hate and wish I couldn't hear right now, but I can't stop myself even if I tried. It's official and I accept it: this Christmas, I'm that crazy woman who can't keep her shit together.

"Fuck, Lily—"

"Don't you say it, King. I'm not in the mood to hear it today."

"Well it's fucking true, so maybe you need to hear it."

Apparently Christmas brings out the crazy in me. Not just this year, but every year. Or so King likes to tell me. My family backs him on this and call it the Christmas Crazies. And while I might accept that this year I'm a crazy woman—*because of people and circumstances outside of my control*—I don't need to hear King go on about it like it's a freaking given every year.

"I'll tell you what I need to hear. I need to hear you say you'll definitely be home for our Christmas dinner tonight. That's it. I'll take care of everything else that still needs to be done for tomorrow and I'll make sure the swing set is built so long as you just get home." I pause for a moment and my voice softens as I add, "I need you here, King."

Silence for a beat before he says, "I'll be there. Everything is taken care of for tomorrow and I'll build that swing set tonight. I don't want you to worry about any of that shit; I've got it covered."

And just like that, the tightening in my chest eases. As much as he tests me and argues with me and pushes my limits, my husband never lets me down. When he says he'll do something, he'll move heaven and hell to deliver on his promise. I just needed to hear him say it.

"I love you."

"I'll be on the road all day." That's King speak for "don't fucking call me unless it's urgent".

"I'll see you tonight."

The line goes dead as he ends the call. I've only got one more thing to tell him.

ME: I hope you're planning on being home for many days. I have many filthy things I want you to do to me.

. . .

"HE'LL BE HOME FOR DINNER?" Zara asks.

Knowing King won't reply to my text, I place my phone down and do my best to concentrate on the day ahead rather than on the fact I miss him so much. "Yes."

"Good."

Tatum starts to say something but there's another knock at the front door.

"Girlfriend," Monroe says when I let her in, "your husband outranks mine for bossiest man alive."

I take the bags of groceries she shoves at me. "We knew this already, Roe. He outranks every man alive when it comes to that."

"Well he reached a new limit with me today. Ask me where I'm supposed to be right now? And then ask me why I'm not there."

"Oh God, what did he boss you into?"

"You're supposed to be at the hairdresser now," Tatum says.

Monroe nods. "Yes, I am, and yet after arguing with King for a good few minutes over it, I agreed to cancel my appointment so I could go grocery shopping. On fucking Christmas Eve. You girls know I hate grocery shopping at the best of times, but the day before Christmas is the absolute worst. Let the record show, I will not be talking to King anytime soon."

"You gave up your hair appointment for this?" I ask, but it's not really a question because I know she did. What I'm stunned at is that she agreed to it. Monroe gives up her hair appointments for no one.

"Let the record also show," she says, the look in her eyes softening a touch, "that I did not do this for King. I did this for you. I know how stressed you've been the last couple of days with everything going on; you do not need to be anywhere near the supermarket today."

"Well let the record show that I love you in ways you can't even comprehend right now. And you are absolutely right; if I'd had to go grocery shopping today, I may have lost any sanity I have left."

She reaches for my hand and squeezes it. "I got you, sister. And let's be honest, I didn't really need to get my hair done today. It's only been two weeks since I saw the hairdresser."

"I know, but still, getting it done is a Christmas tradition for you."

She shrugs. "I'm starting a new Christmas tradition this year: twelve days of not talking to King. I think I'm gonna like my new tradition much more."

I laugh at that. There are days I'd like to start that tradition too.

"Where are the kids?" Tatum asks Monroe.

"Mum has Sage, and Hyde has Parker. Hyde got home just after five yesterday afternoon and Parker hasn't left his side since. He's been missing his daddy." Monroe's three-year-old son is the spitting image of his father and adores Hyde more than Cade adores King. And that's saying something, because my son lives for his father.

Monroe eyes Tatum. "I have more in the car. Can you help me bring everything in?"

"I'll help too," I offer.

"Are the kids okay without you?"

"I've only got Cade home with me this morning and Zara's keeping an eye on him. Mum took pity on me earlier and said she'd have Meredith and Travis for most of the day."

"Okay, let's do this and then I'm thinking you should make me a G&T with more G than T. God knows I need it after stepping foot inside Coles today. And why does it have to be so fucking hot at Christmas? Doesn't the universe understand that cooking all the food we have to cook, and dealing with all the kid stuff we have to deal with, and all the husband bullshit we have to put up with would be so much more bearable if we weren't sweating our asses off?"

"Yeah," Tatum says, "I think maybe we'll just skip the tonic altogether in your drink."

We make our way outside to Monroe's car at the same time one of the club's vans pulls into the driveway. Kick jumps out with a grin on his face. "Ladies," he greets us, and then to me, he says, "I've got the drinks for tomorrow. Where do you want it all?"

"Downstairs in the bar. The back door is open. Do you want a hand?"

He shakes his head as he eyes Fury's bike. "No, you keep doing whatever you were doing. I'll get Fury to help me."

"I'll let him know you need help."

"Thanks, Lily," he says before heading to the back of the van to unload boxes of alcohol and soft drink.

I leave Monroe and Tatum to go in search of Fury and find him out on the back deck cleaning the air conditioning filter.

"I swear King only cleaned that recently," I say.

He glances at me. "Yeah, it's not too bad, but I figured I'd clean it while I'm looking at it all. This isn't the problem, though."

"You've figured out what's wrong?"

"No, it's beyond my knowledge, but I've called a guy I know and he'll be here in the next couple of hours to take a look."

"That is the second-best thing I've heard all day."

He turns quiet for a moment before saying, "King's hopeful this shit in Melbourne will end soon."

Fury's a lot like King in many ways, and his ability to read a situation well is one of their biggest similarities. He's made a point of checking in on me every time he's home from Melbourne. Making sure I'm doing okay with the kids and coping with King being away so much. Some days he's been my saving grace, taking some of my load while giving me a few hours to myself.

I nod at what he's said. "Yeah, I know." Then quietly, in barely a whisper, as if this will make it seem not as real as if I say it louder, I share my current greatest fear. "But this war has been going on for so long now that I wonder if it will ever end. And we've lost too many men.... I can't lose King, Fury. I can't." Tears rush to the surface, and I try hard to force them back into hiding, but I fail. They stream down my face as all the pressure and stress and worry that's been building for far too long refuses to remain buried a second longer.

Fury pulls me into a hug, his strong arms providing me comfort in a moment when I'll take any offered. "You're not going to lose King, Lily. Fuck, he's been shot enough times now and survived that it's fair to say nothing keeps that man down for long."

I look up at him, my heart beating faster than it has in a long time as I contemplate the fact my husband isn't invincible, even though he seems to think he is. "He's exhausted, physically and mentally. Every time he comes home, there's a new piece of him missing. I'm watching the man I love lose far too much, and in the process, he's slowly losing himself." I struggle to get my words out in between my sobs. "I need this war to end because I need my husband not to lose any more of himself."

Fury tightens his arms around me and allows my tears to fall in silence. When I get myself under control, I step out of his hug and say, "Thank you."

"You're a strong woman, Lily, but even the strong crack at times. You need to let yourself crack more often. And ask for help. Zara tells me all the time that you barely ask her for help. She's always ready to pitch in when you need her. And me too when I'm home."

Smiling, I say, "I'm so glad she has you. How are the wedding plans going? I haven't had a chance to catch up with her on them this week."

He arches his brows. "Don't change the subject. Tell me you'll reach out more and then I'll tell you about the wedding."

My smile grows. "I promise I'll reach out more."

"Good."

"Well? The wedding?"

"We finally set a date last night: the twenty-third of March. And I don't give a fuck if this war is still going on then. I'm not waiting any longer for it to end to make Zara my wife."

Fury wanted to marry Zara as soon as he

proposed, but she wanted to wait for everything with the club to have settled down. He's been not-so-patiently waiting. I like that he's put his foot down. My daughter can be stubborn like me; sometimes we need our men to take charge and show us what we actually need rather than what we're telling ourselves we need.

"Okay, now that you've given me some good news that I can focus on rather than all the bad, I came to let you know that Kick is out the front and wants you to help him unload the drinks for tomorrow," I say.

"Will do," he says, and I make my way to the door to go back inside. As I'm entering the house, I turn back to him. "Tell me you got Zara two presents for tomorrow. She's funny about only receiving one present to cover both Christmas and her birthday."

He grins. "I've got it sorted."

I should have known he would.

As I move through the house in search of the girls, I think about everything going on with my family and the club. And about what Fury said. He's right: I do need to ask for help more often, especially if things in Melbourne don't change soon. King has hardly been home this year, and when he has, he's been busy trying to give the kids the time they need, the house the attention it needs, and the club what it needs. Our relationship has taken a back seat and I've been okay with that because I understand everything at stake. Through it all, I've worked hard to handle stuff on my own in an effort to not burden King with more than he already has, but my current level of neurotic behaviour can't be ignored.

Something needs to give and I need to make that happen.

2

Lily

"*L*ily darling, I'm not convinced we have enough food for all the people coming for dinner," my mother says. It's just after 5:00 p.m. and we're preparing for our yearly Christmas Eve family dinner tonight. "Between our family and King's family, that's a lot of people."

I take a deep breath. "At this point, Mum, I just won't eat if we don't have enough, and neither will you." I actually don't agree with my mother's assessment, but arguing with her is a waste of time.

"Lil," my sister Brynn calls out from the dining

room, "can you come in here and give me a hand, please?"

Without acknowledging the look on her face at what I just said, I say to my mother, "Can you please check the roast while I help Brynn? And if Jamie comes in, ask him how the ham is going?" I've put my sister's husband on ham duty since King isn't here. He's spent most of his time here this afternoon outside, alternating between tidying up the lawn and garden for me, swimming, and barbecuing the ham.

After Mum agrees, I head into the dining room, grateful to leave the hot kitchen behind. Fury's air conditioning guy fixed the air con about two hours ago and it's heaven in the house now, but the kitchen remains warm because we've had the oven going for hours.

Brynn's eyes meet mine the minute I join her and she smiles. It's the smile of a conspirator. "I don't really need you. I just knew you'd be at your limit with Mum by now."

I drop down onto one of the dining room seats. "You are the best little sister in the world and I love you more than anyone."

She takes a seat across from me. "More than King?"

"Right now, yes." It's a lie, but we joke about this often and Brynn knows just how much I truly do love her.

"Any update on what time he'll be home?"

"No. I'm taking that as a sign he'll be here for dinner."

"Okay, so you know I'm on board with you trying to be calmer, but I kinda think we need to prepare you in case he doesn't make it for dinner."

After Fury told me to ask for help more often, I called Brynn and begged her to come and spend the day helping Zara and me. I didn't need to beg; she was more than ready to do as I asked. Monroe and Tatum stayed for a while too, and helped me set up for tomorrow. Hailee and Evie popped over as well, and with everyone's help, I have everything under control for Christmas. Cade even came through for me and cleaned up his room.

"The Christmas Crazies have disappeared, Brynny. You don't have to worry about me."

"I'm more worried for King."

"Mummy!" Meredith runs into the room and flings herself at me, distraught. "Travis won't let me have my book!"

"Which book?"

"The one Daddy gave me!"

I place my hands on her arms. "Daddy has given you a lot of books, Meredith. Why don't you choose a different one to read?"

"No! I want *Matilda*."

This now makes sense to me. King gave *Matilda* to her the last time he was home. She's barely let go of it since then.

Brynn stands and moves around the table to us. Reaching for Meredith's hand, she says, "Come with me, baby. We'll get your book off Travis."

I shoot her a look of appreciation and watch the two of them exit the room. Less than a minute later, Mum sticks her head around the corner. "Darling, we need to make this trifle."

"Yeah, we do." I follow her into the kitchen, ignoring the ache in my feet and wishing I'd chosen a much faster dessert to make than the chocolate trifle I found online a few days ago. However, I chose this because trifle is King's favourite dessert and there's no way I'm not making it for him. Spoiling my husband with his favourite food is something I love to do. Even on the days I want to smother him.

Mum and I spend the next hour and a half assembling the trifle, finishing off the roast pork and veggies, making sure the ham is cooked perfectly, and getting everything ready for dinner. Brynn and Jamie organise the kids. Zara and Fury arrive, and my daughter surprises me with a chocolate pavlova with spiced pears and butterscotch sauce she made.

"Oh my God, Zara, this looks divine!" I gush as I take a good look at it. "Thank you!"

"She practiced it the other night," Fury says. "I can tell you it tastes as good as it looks."

"Holy shit, Zara," Holly says, joining us. "Can we just skip straight to dessert?"

I motion for Holly to come to me. "Get over here and give me a hug, baby girl. I feel like I haven't seen you for years."

She rolls her eyes but does as I say. "I was away for a month, Mum."

I wrap my arms around her and squeeze tightly, not wanting to let her go. "Yes, and it felt like years to me."

She extricates herself from my hold. "I hate to tell you but I think I have the travel bug now. I'm already planning my next trip."

"Oh God, please tell me this one is to a safer destination than where you've just been." After spending the last month worrying not only about King and the club, but also about Holly who was traipsing around countries that any mother would prefer their child not to visit, I'm not sure I can survive that again.

"Relax, Mother, I'm looking at Canada for my next trip."

Before I can respond, the back door opens and Skylar enters the house with her current boyfriend, Tristan. I wasn't sure if he was coming because the last time he attended a family gathering, King was an asshole to him. I like the guy and am impressed he's come back for more.

Skylar's eyes meet mine and she smiles big. "Your air con is working again!"

I hug her. When I pull away, I smile at Tristan. "Hey, Tristan. Good to see you." After he returns my greeting, I look back at Skylar, touching her hair. "I love, love, love this cut on you. When did you get it done?" She's cut her long hair and it now sits just below her ears.

"Last night. I've never gone this short before, but this damn heat inspired me."

"I love it, too," Zara says.

Skylar takes Tristan's hand and moves further into the kitchen so she can catch up with Zara and Holly. Travis and Meredith run in to join us, having heard their aunt's voice. Cade follows shortly after, and suddenly I need some space. There are too many people in here for me.

Leaving them, I make my way to my bedroom at the front of the house. I have a new red dress to wear tonight, and I want to quickly tidy up my hair and face.

I've got the dress on, my hair sorted and am halfway through my make-up when I hear the rumble of King's bike outside. I know it's his and not anyone else's because, after eight years of being married to him, I could pick his bike out anywhere.

Hoping the kids haven't heard him—because I desperately want to steal a few moments alone with him—I quietly let myself out of the house and hurry down the stairs to where he's parking the bike in the garage.

It's been just over three weeks since King has been home. We've spoken every day, but some of those conversations were rushed because he's been occupied with club stuff. These three weeks have been the worst of the entire year for me. I don't know if that's because things have been more intense with the club, resulting in King feeling distracted and disconnected from us, or whether I'm just so exhausted that I'm not coping as well as I usually do. Either way, I'm glad he's home now.

Complete overwhelm consumes me as I watch him take his helmet off and turn my way. Relief floods my body and tears threaten. I don't let them fall, though; that's the last thing he needs on his plate.

King looks as tired as I feel, and yet the closer I get to him, I see the spark of heat in his eyes. That same heat pools low in my belly.

God, how I love my husband.

Regardless of how little energy we both have left in the tank, I know tonight is going to be spent getting our fill.

He reaches for me, gripping my arm and pulling

me hard against him. No words are exchanged between us; the only sound filling the hot night air is the buzz of cicadas singing their song.

Every ounce of tension in my body falls away as King does the thing he always does when he comes home. His hands and eyes roam over my body. It's his way of checking no harm has come to me while he's been away. He does it with the kids too.

When his eyes find mine again, the desire blazing in them pushes me over the edge. I curl my hand around his neck and hook a leg around his. I need to be in his arms with all my limbs wrapped around him.

He knows my needs—we've done this dance thousands of times during our marriage—and slides his hand under my ass so he can pull me into his arms.

Our lips crash together and my body hums with the kind of electricity only King creates. His deep growl of satisfaction vibrates through me as he carries me from the garage to the connecting entertainment area and into the bathroom in there.

Kicking the door shut behind him, he drags his mouth from mine and rasps, "Fuck me, I've missed you."

It's not often King expresses his feelings in this way. I know he misses me, but he rarely tells me.

I reach for his belt the moment he places me on

the vanity, my mind warring over whether to have a conversation over him missing me or whether to fuck him. Sex wins—it usually does—and it turns out that while King may have uttered those words, he also has no intention of carrying on a conversation.

His hands are under my dress before I've managed to undo his belt.

My panties are on the floor before I even get to the button on his jeans.

He's bent down to run his tongue along my pussy before I realise what's happening.

My fingers tangle in his hair as I arch my back and express my pleasure.

I'm going to come faster than I ever have. Three weeks without him and I'm a mess of frantic need.

My orgasm builds as he works his tongue in all the ways I love. When he reaches for my hand and directs my fingers to my pussy, I almost shatter. I don't, though. I manage to hold myself back, wanting him to take me to the edge and back, over and over before I finally allow myself to come.

Sliding my finger inside me, he finds my eyes and watches as he pushes one of his in too. He dips his mouth to my clit, still watching me, and tongues it.

My eyes flutter shut as I pant through the orgasm that wants release. The pleasure is intense and I want to let myself go, let myself feel it all, right now, but what I want more is for King to increase it to greater heights.

"Lily," he growls, reaching our fingers deeper inside. "Look at me. Watch me fuck you."

I obey his command at the same time the sound of people running filters through from above us.

The kids have worked out their daddy is home. That understanding flares in King's eyes and he curses under his breath.

Letting me go, he finishes what I started with his jeans and reaches for his dick while I scramble off the vanity and turn around.

He takes hold of my neck while meeting my gaze in the mirror and thrusting hard inside me.

"*Fuck*." The word falls from both our lips as he finds his rhythm. As the footsteps above us make their way to the front door.

I grip the edge of the vanity.

King has never felt so good. That's what three weeks without him will do to a woman.

His fingers around my neck tighten the closer we move towards release.

The footsteps are on the stairs now.

The sound of the kids' excitement becomes audible.

King pounds hard and fast into me.

I'm consumed by him.

Barely able to think about anything or anyone but him and this moment right here.

The footsteps are closer.

The excited chatter grows louder.

The kids are nearly here.

King is inside me, giving me himself, but I already feel him slipping away again.

I love our kids, but it's at times like this I wish I didn't have to share him.

"Oh God," I cry as I orgasm, wanting, needing way more time with him than I've had.

He thrusts one last time and stills as he comes.

His hand stays around my throat while his arm circles me, squeezing me to him.

Kissing my neck, he says, "I've fucking missed you."

"Daddy! Daddy!" Meredith's voice sounds from the garage.

King pulls out of me and we quickly clean up before leaving the bathroom.

He's barely stepped foot in the garage when Meredith flings herself at him. Travis follows suit and attaches himself to one of his father's legs. Cade isn't far behind, but now that he's seven, he's more restrained and holds himself back. But it's clear in his eyes he's relieved to see his father home.

Brynn enters the garage and looks at me apologetically. Moving closer, she says softly, "I tried to keep them upstairs."

I smile. "Thanks." With one last look at King and the kids, I say to her, "Let's go get dinner on the table."

I'm surrounded by nearly all my family tonight. Robbie begged to be allowed to have dinner with his girlfriend's family, and Annika and her family are with her husband's parents, but everyone else is here. Tomorrow we'll celebrate with the club, our extended family. And if it's the last thing I do, I'll push all my current worries from my mind and focus on the good in our life. My kids are safe and happy, and my husband is home. And that's everything I need.

3

Lily

Stepping out of the shower, I reach for my towel and dry myself off. Not that I really need to, the stifling heat that's still heavy in the air even at 1:00 a.m. is enough to do that job for me. And I thought the air con had been fixed. Turned out, it hasn't, and halfway through dinner, it stopped working again.

Dressing in the sheer red baby-doll I bought for tonight, I head out to the back deck and down the stairs to where King's building the swing set. He came out here about two hours ago after everyone left and has refused to let me help.

He stops when he hears me and glances up, his eyes going straight to my breasts. Eight years have passed since we met, and every time he looks at me like this still feels like the first time. I didn't have this in my first marriage, and I thank God daily that I have it with King. Even when he's pissing me off so damn much I could do damage to him.

"How much longer do you think until you'll be done?" I ask when I reach him.

"Half an hour. Maybe."

"You should let me help. We'll get it done quicker."

"No. Go to bed. You're exhausted."

"And you're not? Besides, there's no way either of us are sleeping tonight and you know that." A shot of desire races through me at the thought.

"Lily," he starts, his voice all bossy and gruff like he's about to order me around. I cut him off, though; I'm in no mood to be bossed. Not unless it's in the bedroom.

"You've been away for three weeks and that quick fuck earlier comes nowhere near touching my need for you. Just let me help already so I can have you."

His nostrils flare and he reaches out to take hold of my neck. "You're not fucking helping me. You've run this place for three weeks without me; the least I can fucking do is build a swing set."

"It's not like you've sat on your ass for three weeks doing nothing. We're a team, King. I didn't have kids with you thinking shit would be easy all the time."

"Yeah, but you sure as fuck didn't have kids with me thinking you'd go through a year like the one we're having."

I frown. "What's wrong?"

"Nothing. I'm just trying to get you—"

"Bullshit. Something's off. First you tell me you missed me. Twice. You never tell me that. And now you're doing everything but fucking me, and we both know that is not like you at all. Talk to me."

His fingers dig into my skin as he squeezes my neck. "I've thought of your cunt every fucking day I've been away. Fucking you is the highest fucking priority I have right now, but for once in my life, I'm trying to think of someone other than myself." He slides his free hand under the hem of my baby-doll. "I've never seen you so tired, and what I want to do to you will wipe you the fuck out." He skims his hand up my body over my stomach to my breasts before growling, "The only thing off with me is that I'm holding myself back from slamming my dick so fucking hard inside you that it'll break you."

Oh God.

I want to finish the conversation I began, because

I don't believe there's nothing wrong with him, but when he talks filthy to me and puts his hands on me, I'm helpless but to go along for the ride. Especially when he's giving me what I'm starving for.

"Wipe me out, King," I beg, desperate for him to fuck me exactly how he mentioned. "Stop holding yourself back."

"Fuck, Lily," he growls, looking torn. "It's fucking Christmas tomorrow and the last thing I want is you too exhausted for the kids."

The way things usually go down when King comes home after being away is we have a marathon session of sex and then I sleep for most of the next day while he hangs out with the kids. So I understand where he's coming from, but Goddammit, I want him.

Now.

Tonight.

For the entire night.

I need to be with my husband in the way that truly connects us.

Pushing my body against his, the words "I need this" fall from my mouth in an urgent and fierce rush. My eyes search his, wondering what's gotten into him. In all our years of marriage, I can't recall one time he's held back like this.

He turns silent for a beat, and I see the conflict he's struggling with.

Fuck, maybe we should spend tonight talking.

The thought flitters away as fast as it came. I know him as well as I know myself, and King needs a couple of days at home after being away before he'll start talking.

Finally he nods and says, "Let me finish this and then—"

He's cut off when Travis's voice floats down from the back deck. "Mummy, I'm sick."

King's head jerks up to look at our son. "Fuck," he mutters as he lets me go and makes a move to head upstairs.

I grab his arm and stop him. "You finish the swing set. I'll take care of Travis." I say this like taking care of Travis will be quick, but we both know it won't be. Travis is the needy one of our children; when he's sick, he demands our complete attention.

King looks at me with regret, his eyes communicating what I already know: there won't be any sex now.

He nods. "I'll be up soon."

I leave him and run up the stairs to Travis. Scooping him into my arms, I take a good look at him. "You don't look well, baby. What's wrong?"

His little hands come to my neck and he grasps me tightly. "My tummy is sore."

I only needed to take one look at him to know he's going to vomit and he's just confirmed it, so I take him into the bathroom. Sitting on the edge of the bath, I deposit him on the floor and say, "Do you feel like you're going to be sick?"

He nods, his lips quivering. "Yes."

I turn him to face the toilet and say, "Okay, we'll wait here and see—"

Before I finish what I'm saying, he retches violently into the toilet and then starts crying, his tiny body shaking.

I move behind him, rubbing his back and holding him.

He vomits three more times, growing more upset each time. Once I think he's gotten it all out of his system, I clean him up and then carry him into his bedroom.

As I lie him down, he grabs for my neck again as tears stream down his face. "Don't leave, Mummy! My tummy's sore still."

I sit on the bed with him and try to calm him. "I know, baby. I'm not going anywhere."

"You promise?" The tremble in his voice slays me. I hate watching any of my children go through sickness.

I nod. "I promise. Wiggle across so I can lie with you."

A minute later, he's cuddled up to me and I'm pretty sure I'm not far off passing out now that I've stopped and lain down. King's right: I'm absolutely shattered.

I don't fall asleep, though. Travis is agitated, so I sing his favourite songs to him in an effort to get him off to sleep. I have no idea how long I do this for but it feels like quite a long time. It's not until King steps into the bedroom that I stop singing. Travis is asleep but I kept going because he has a habit of stirring easily if I stop straight away.

"Is he okay?" King asks.

"He vomited a few times, but he's been asleep for a little while now so I think he's settled. I'm going to stay a bit longer though. Just in case."

"I'll have a shower and then take over."

"No, I want you to get some sleep tonight."

"This isn't up for negotiation," he says as determination fixes itself to his expression.

When King gives me the look he's currently giving me, I know not to bother arguing, so I don't. I simply nod and watch him as he exits the room, wondering how many days I've got him home for this time. Praying that it's longer than he usually stays in between trips lately.

I lie with Travis, waiting for King to shower and return. However, after deciding I need to know now how long he intends to stay, I go in search of him.

As I enter our room, King walks out of the en

suite, a towel hanging low on his hips, his chest bare. Raking his fingers through his still-wet hair, he comes to me. "He's asleep?"

"Yeah." His chest has my complete attention and I momentarily forget what I came here to ask him.

He tips my chin up and asks, "What?"

Still distracted by his chest. "Huh?"

"You have that look on your face that tells me you've got something on your mind. What is it?"

Right. "How long will you be home?"

"I'm not sure."

"Yeah, but what's your estimate?" He always has an estimate and I've learned to subtract a day or so from it because nine times out of ten, something urgent comes up that he has to go back for.

He looks pained as he drags time out before giving me his answer. "It may be the day after tomorrow."

"Boxing Day?" Surely I've heard him incorrectly.

"Yeah."

"Oh. Okay." I stumble over my words because this was not at all what I was expecting. Although I should have been because the situation in Melbourne has been intensifying for weeks.

He scrubs a hand over his face, his eyes betraying his frustration. "Fuck, Lily, I wish I could tell you a different timeframe, but I can't."

I nod, swallowing my disappointment. Trying to at least, because at this point, I'm too tired and emotional to actually manage that. "I know. And I get it. I do. But I'm worried about the kids. Especially Cade."

"Why? What's going on with him?"

"His behaviour is out of control."

"I'll have a talk with him about it."

I turn silent. Talking to Cade about his behaviour won't fix anything if the reason why he's acting out doesn't change. But I don't want to lump that on King. Not when he's fighting for his club and everyone's safety.

Moving into me, he takes hold of my face with both hands. I'm intoxicated by his scent, his bare skin, his proximity. Instantly. Because that's what King does to me. "We're gonna be all right. Shit in Melbourne will be sorted soon."

I curl my hands over his biceps and ask the one question I'm almost too scared to ask. The one question I've never broached. "What if it's not, King? What if this drags on for another six months or another year?"

He doesn't answer me straight away, and I can tell by the flicker of his eyes that this is something he's thought about a lot, too. "Winter and I are making damn sure it won't." His mood changes swiftly and his eyes darken as he lifts me into his arms. Walking me backwards, he drops me on the bed and positions himself over me. "There's no fucking way I can go on for another six months or year being away from you all the time."

My hands go to his chest and then run down his body as he brings his mouth to mine. I flick his towel open and remove it while our tongues tangle together. When I stroke his cock, he growls deeply and reaches a hand under my baby-doll. A moment later, his fingers are inside me, and another growl comes from deep inside him.

Pulling his lips from mine, he rasps, "Fuck." He then moves down my body, spreads my legs, and buries his face in my pussy.

Dear. God.

I grip the sheets and arch my back as he gives me what I need.

His mouth.

His tongue.

His love.

And just as I'm losing myself in the pleasure, Travis screams out for me.

King responds instantly, letting me go and moving off the bed. Looking down at me with regret, he says, "I'll go."

I lift myself up onto my elbows. "We're not having sex tonight, are we?"

He throws clothes on and says, "No," before bending to kiss me again. "Go to sleep."

I watch him until I can't see him anymore and wonder if we'll get our time together before he has to return to Melbourne. At the rate we're going, I'm beginning to seriously doubt it.

4

Zara

"Daddy! Wake up! We've got presents!"

I crack an eye open and find Noah crawling over his father, shaking him to wake him from the deep sleep he's in.

Since Fury arrived home from Melbourne four days ago, he's slept better than he ever has. His insomnia is nowhere to be seen. Not that I expect that to be a forever thing, but I love all the sleep he's getting this week.

"Noah," I say. "Come here, little man. You can show me where all the presents are."

As I sit and swing my legs over the bed to head

out into the lounge room with Noah, Fury's arm hooks around my waist. "You're not going anywhere, princess."

Noah had crawled off his father, but at the sound of his voice, his little eyes light up and he exclaims, "Daddy! Presents!"

I laugh as Fury drags me close. Rolling to face him, I trace the curve of his smile with my gaze. Seeing pure happiness on his face makes me happier than ever. We've been together for five months, and each day I feel more blessed than the day before to have him in my life.

Looking at his son, Fury says, "Where are these presents?"

"Under the tree!" Noah loves everything about Christmas and that makes me love it even more. His glee is infectious.

"Okay," Fury says, "you go and figure out which one you want to open first. Zara and I will be out in a minute."

He does as his father says, and once we're alone, Fury rolls to face me. Placing his leg over mine, he takes hold of my face. "I had plans for you this morning, but I fucked that up by sleeping in." Dropping a kiss to my lips, he then says, "Happy birthday, beautiful."

I grasp his arm. "Tell me more about these plans."

"Fuck no. I've gotta go open presents with my son; the last thing I need right now is the hard-on that would give me."

Grinning, I say, "At least promise me a raincheck."

His lips brush mine again. "Baby, there'll be a raincheck and then some tonight."

I wish it was already tonight. I mean, I'm looking forward to celebrating Christmas with my family and the club today, but what I'd love even more is spending the entire day alone with my man.

Pushing his chest, I say, "Okay, you need to leave this room now or else I may never let you leave and I think Noah will stop liking me if that happens."

"Nothing could make that kid stop liking you. He asked me on the phone yesterday if you'd be here today. When I told him you're living here now, he practically exploded with excitement." He arches his brow, giving me his "I told you so" expression.

Smacking him playfully, I say, "I get it, you were right, but I still wanted to give him these months to get used to me being around."

Fury wanted me to move in with him as soon as we got together. He tried his best to boss me into it and hasn't let up over the past four months, but I held my ground. I didn't want to force myself onto his son; I wanted us to take our time and get a good feel for each other. I also wanted that time to date

Fury. To get to know each other after four years of not being in each other's life. I was scared that rushing straight into living with him might put too much pressure on our new relationship.

He grins as he moves off the bed. "Let's be honest. You were still taking that test drive, weren't you? Making sure I lived up to your expectations."

I shrug as I stand and head for the en suite. "Maybe."

He closes the distance between us and backs me up against the wall, his hands all over me. The man can't keep them to himself. "I'm taking it I passed."

A smile tugs at my lips. "I guess you could read that into the situation. But don't forget I still have my apartment until I find someone to take over the lease. Maybe I'm still test driving you." I grind myself against him. "Maybe you should remain on your best behaviour. For instance, I'm not opposed to having a man slave."

He groans as I press myself against him. "You play dirty, woman."

"You love it dirty."

Letting me go, he backs away, looking pained. "I only like it when I can do something with it."

Lifting my chin at the door, I say, "Go and see your son. I'll be out in a minute."

Reaching for my arm, he draws me close again. He slides a hand along my jawbone and threads his fingers into my hair. "I love you" falls from his lips before he claims one last kiss.

I expect a short kiss, but he deepens it, and if I'm reading him right, struggles to end it. When we finally come up for air, I'm breathless and panting a little. "I love you, too."

His eyes search mine for a long few moments, and without another word, he exits the room, leaving me a wanting mess of need.

Goddam, it's going to be a long day.

Five minutes later, after I've freshened up, I find Fury and Noah in the lounge room. Noah looks like he's about to burst with excitement and impatience as he holds the biggest present that was under the tree.

I sit next to Fury on the couch as he says to Noah, "Okay, you can open it now."

We spend the next twenty minutes opening presents and watching as Noah loses himself in the joy of discovering each present. Fury has spoiled him a little this year. I imagine his ex wouldn't be too impressed to see how many presents Noah received —because she made it clear to him her thoughts on spoiling their son—but I get it. Fury feels a lot of guilt over being away so much. He told me he knows he went overboard on the presents, but I told him to give himself grace. There's no perfect way to parent and he's simply doing the best he can.

As Noah sits surrounded by his presents, seemingly unable to decide which one to play with first, Fury whispers against my ear, "Are you ready for your birthday presents?"

"You bought me more than one?"

"I do recall you telling me years ago that you're not okay with receiving one present to cover both Christmas and your birthday, so I covered all my bases by buying way more than one present. I figure this might protect me if I fuck up one year and only get you one."

Something tells me Fury won't ever fuck that up, but I wanna keep him on his toes, so I say, "Nope. Fair warning: nothing will protect you if you do that."

He shakes his head playfully. "You know how to work your man hard."

I loop my hands around his neck. "Am I gonna see these presents or are we just going to sit here and talk about them?"

Scooping me into his arms, he lifts me and says to Noah, "Come with us, Noah. We're gonna show Zara her birthday present."

Noah's head jerks up and his eyes blaze with enthusiasm. Pushing himself up off the floor, he says, "Ooh, trees, trees!"

Fury chuckles and says, "Shh, it's a secret, remember?"

Noah's eyes widen as his hand crashes over his mouth.

Fury lets me down and reaches for his son's hand. "It's all good, but let's not ruin the whole surprise, okay?"

I'm so intrigued as to what this present could be and that's only heightened when the two of them lead me out to the front yard.

Noah lets go of his father's hand and runs across the lawn to the corner garden he and Fury have been working on for a couple of weeks. "Zara! Come look!"

"I love his excitement," I say to Fury before hurrying to where Noah is waiting for me.

As I draw closer, I realise what they got me for my birthday: a garden. This garden they've been working on together.

Fury comes up behind me and slips his arms around my waist. Bending his mouth to my ear, he says, "Happy birthday."

I place a hand over his at my waist. "You really think I can keep these plants alive?"

"You've kept one plant alive this year. I think you're ready for this next level."

"It's going to be pink!" Noah says as he walks all around the garden inspecting the plants.

"These plants weren't here yesterday," I say to

Fury as I turn in his arms. "Did you plant them last night?"

He smiles. "Yeah."

"That's why you slept in. What time did you come to bed?"

I'd kept him awake for hours after we arrived home from Mum's dinner. I can only imagine how little sleep he's had.

"Don't worry about my sleep." His hand lands on my ass and he pulls me closer. "What you need to start thinking about are all the ways you're gonna show me how much you love this garden."

I love it when he's playful like this. Each time he comes home from Melbourne, it takes him a couple of days to shake off the dark mood the club war shrouds him in. I give him the space to do that and I'm always then blessed with this side of him.

"Trust me, I have lots of things on my list, but I'm a little concerned my man might be too tired for any of them tonight. We may need to let you rest for a few days."

"Daddy, let Zara go. I wanna show her the plants," Noah says, his voice taking on the insistent tone that means we have less than a minute before he hounds us to give him all our attention.

Fury ignores his son for another few moments and keeps his gaze pinned to mine. What he's communicating in his eyes causes a whoosh of flutters in my belly. "You should know by now that I don't rest." He brings his mouth to my ear again and says just loud enough for me to hear, "The minute I drop Noah off this morning, we're getting started on your list. And I don't give a fuck if that means we're late to lunch."

"Daddy!" Noah says, grabbing Fury's arm and pulling hard.

Fury lets me go, and after one last lingering look at me, he finally gives Noah the attention he wants. "How about you tell Zara about the plants we chose for her, little man?"

This makes Noah happy and he attempts to give me a rundown on the plants. When he stumbles over some of the names, Fury helps him out. By the time they finish talking, I feel even more love for these two than I already felt. They not only built this garden together, but they also listened to me every time we went to the nursery, taking note of the plants I liked. And when Fury tells me one last thing about the garden, I'm sure my heart will explode with love for him.

Pointing at the camellia sasanquas he's planted —a plant I really love—he says, "There're five of those. One for every birthday since we met."

I stare at him, speechless for a good few moments. I've never had a man in my life as thoughtful as he is. When I finally find my words, I say, "I love you and I'm pretty sure you're now protected if you ever screw up with my birthday and Christmas presents," before crashing my lips to his and showing him how much I love my present.

When the kiss ends, he says, "You know I'm never fucking that up, Zara. I intend to be yours forever, so I'm never fucking anything up."

It's not even 8:00 a.m. and this is already my favourite birthday and Christmas ever.

Birdie

"Birdie, have you heard a word I've said to you?" Mum asks early Christmas morning while I stand in her kitchen staring at the kettle waiting for it to boil. She's been prattling on about her latest dating adventure, and while I did start out paying attention, my thoughts drifted off when she got to the bit about the guy still working in the same job for the same company for the past thirty-five years. I mean, who does that?

"Yes, I'm listening," I lie.

She plants her hands on her hips and gives me her "you're lying" look. "You were not."

I stare back at her trying to win this little detour in conversation, but I know it's pointless. "Seriously, how is he not bored out of his brain still doing the same job for all these decades?"

"Seriously, why are you focussing on that rather than the fact he wants me to wear leather, strap on a collar, and submit to whatever he tells me to do?"

I almost choke on my own tongue. "Jesus, are you going to?" Not that I'm against a little BDSM if that's what people are into, but my mother? I can't even imagine it. She'd likely smack him away if he tried to dominate her.

Her eyes widen. "Darling, I like a strong man, but if I ever tell you I have a safe word, have me committed."

"You have a safe word?" Winter says to Mum as he enters the kitchen and catches the end of our conversation. He appears as perplexed with the idea as I was.

"God, no," Mum says. "But the guy I've been dating wants me to."

"You gonna keep seeing him?" Winter asks.

"Not if I can help it," Mum says.

I slide my hand around his waist when he comes to me, and take hold of his face with my other hand so I can pull him down for a kiss. "Merry Christmas," I murmur once I end the kiss. "How was your run?" He's been gone for a good hour and is sweaty as hell, but I don't care. I'll take him any way I can get him. Especially since I've been in Sydney for the last week before he joined me late yesterday afternoon.

He brushes his lips over mine again, whispering, "Fuck, you taste good." Then, pulling away, he says, "The run was good, but it's hot out there. I'm gonna go take a shower."

"Winter," Mum says as he grabs the cold water out of the fridge. "I know you said you're leaving tomorrow, but I'm missing my son-in-law. I've hardly seen you this year. Are you sure you can't stay another few days?"

I make eyes at my mother. We've discussed this and I've made it clear to her not to harass him about staying longer.

She makes eyes back at me. Of course she does; she thinks she can get away with anything when it comes to Winter. He humours her more than anyone, but she's about to find out that on this topic, he humours no one.

The light in his eyes disappears. "No, I can't, Jennifer."

Mum's eyes widen a little. Winter never calls her by her full name anymore. "Not even an extra day? You could go home the day after Boxing—"

Winter's face turns to stone. "I've said no and I mean no. This isn't up for negotiation." He guzzles his glass of water and exits the kitchen without another word to either of us. I take in the set of his shoulders as he leaves; they're hard as stone too.

"Goodness," Mum says, looking like she's just been fully chastised. "I don't recognise him this trip. He's like a whole different man."

Mum hasn't seen Winter in four months. A lot has happened in those months. Plus, it's Christmas and that always brings out his darker side. "Remember it's Christmas, Mum. Max is on his mind at this time of year. And you know he's got the club stuff consuming him at the moment. I told you not to give him hell about this."

"Well, all I can say is I hope things change soon, because I'm concerned you're losing the man you married."

Winter is not the man I married. I lost parts of him years ago when he lost more than anyone should lose in their lifetime. There are pieces of him still in there, but life stole some pieces it shouldn't have. Mum doesn't often get a glimpse into any of this because, like she said, she hardly sees him anymore. And I don't often discuss him with her. Not in this way. She wouldn't understand because she doesn't understand club life. She hears about our fertility battles and my work issues, and random life stuff, but anything to do with the club is kept between Lily and me. She's my go-to person when I need to get that stuff off my chest.

"Please don't bring any of this up with him. I just want us to have a nice Christmas together," I say.

She watches me silently for a few moments before nodding her agreement. Thankfully, she lets the subject go. "Speaking of which, what time do you think you'll be back from your lunch at Lily's? I'm trying to co-ordinate everyone for dinner tonight and I thought it might be nice for us to get together earlier so we can really catch up."

"How about four o'clock? I don't think Winter wants to stay too long at this lunch."

"Can you go and check that time with him so I can confirm it for Lucas and Carey?"

I agree and head into the guest bedroom Winter and I are staying in. I find him in the bathroom standing under the shower with both hands pressed to the tiles and his head bowed. I can't see his face, but I don't need to in order to know he's not in a good place. That information is written all over his body.

This year has been the hardest one we've ever lived through together. And that's saying something because the last eight have been hard. Through it all, we've stayed strong, but I've recently admitted to myself that I think we may need some help with what we're going through now. I'm beginning to think there might be a limit for a couple with what they can cope with, and I think maybe we've reached that limit. I'm worried if we don't seek help, we might slowly unravel, and that's not a place I ever want to get to.

"Hey," I say, not wanting to intrude on his quiet time but also wanting nothing more than to get in the shower with him and wrap my arms around him. To soothe him. To help him move through the pain he's feeling.

He doesn't move except to swing his head to the side and look at me. The torment in his eyes hits me in the chest and I feel it too. God, how I feel it.

We're drowning here.

I can't not be with him, so I pull my clothes off and open the shower door to join him. Placing my hand to his back, I move against him, sliding my body around his so I'm in between him and the shower wall. Winter has packed on a lot of muscle in the last twelve months while pushing himself to get as strong as he can. I think it's been his way of dealing with not only his club battle but also with our personal battle. When I'm this close to him, I feel tiny, and whenever his arms circle me, I feel so damn safe that I don't ever want to be anywhere but in his arms. This time, though, his arms don't come around me. He keeps his hands to the tiles either side of my body and stares down at me, not uttering a word.

"Is it Max?" I ask softly.

His eyes search mine before he pushes off from the tiles. Water from the shower cascades over him and he reaches for the showerhead to redirect it away from him. "Yeah. And the club." Reaching for me, he adds, "And us. Fuck."

The jagged tone of his voice nearly breaks me. Nearly. But I hold my shit together. For him. "Do you want to talk about it?" Winter's not a big talker. Not about his shit, anyway. He loves to get me to talk when I'm going through stuff, but when it comes to him, he shuts down and tries to process his pain alone. I've learned over the years not to force him into talking because it never ends well for us when I do that.

He cups the back of my head and pulls my mouth to his. "No."

His lips claim mine at the same time his hands reach for my ass. When he lifts me, I wrap my arms and legs around him, grateful that we have each other. Grateful that no matter what we've gone through, we've clung to our love.

We lose ourselves in this kiss. After a week apart —because Winter insisted I come to Sydney before him so I could spend time with my family—we reunited last night with the kind of sex that staying at your mother's house allows for. It wasn't bad sex, but it wasn't what we're used to, and God how I'm missing some hot, rough sex with my husband.

"Fuck," he rasps, coming up for air.

Breathless, I grip his face and pull his mouth back to mine. "Don't fucking stop."

Our kiss grows demanding. Urgent. Frantic.

Our bodies are pressed so hard together we could almost be one.

Our need is frenzied.

"Christ, Birdie." Winter lets go of me so he can drop to his knees. Hooking one of my legs over his shoulder, he brings his mouth to my pussy and runs his tongue along it while rubbing his thumb over my clit.

I cry out with pleasure, not even caring if my mother can hear me. I can't censor myself any longer. Gripping his hair, I push the back of his head to keep his face against my pussy. I need more from his tongue. From his beard. From his fingers.

"Oh fuck," I almost scream when he alternates between his tongue inside me and his fingers. And when he works me deep inside with those fingers while running his tongue over and over my clit, I completely abandon myself to the pleasure.

"Oh God, oh God." It becomes a chant.

I squeeze his hair.

I press myself harder against his face.

I pant through my building orgasm.

"Fuck!" This time it's a scream as I shatter. Every nerve ending is lit from the bliss Winter has delivered.

He unhooks my leg from his shoulder and stands. Wiping my cum from his beard, he growls, "We're going back to me doing that every morning. Life's too fucking short not to taste you every day."

I frantically grab for him, needing him inside me. "Can we discuss this after you fuck me?"

Taking hold of my arms, he stops me and crushes his body to mine. The look in his eyes tells me he has something important to say so I give him the space to say it. "I know I've been distracted and distant for a while now, Angel, and I'm sorry. This shit going on... it's fucked up and I've allowed it to come between us. I won't do that anymore."

My heart hurts for him. He thinks this is all on him? It's not. "You're not the only one who's allowed distance to build, Winter. We're both hurting. We both did this."

He works his jaw, determination clear in his eyes. "However it happened, it stops now. You come first, every fucking day from here on out."

I want to tell him that what we need is a whole lot more than sex every day, but I don't want to ruin this moment. Baby steps. We can start with this and build from here. Today, though, we just need to be close and start connecting again.

"I love you and I'll never stop loving you." I kiss him, long and slow. "And now what I really want is for you to fuck me and not hold back."

He doesn't need any further encouragement. Spinning me around, he takes hold of my hips and thrusts inside me. Hard. Exactly how I want it.

When we're finished, he kisses me one last time and says with force, "I love you. Never forget that."

"I never will. And I'll never allow anything to break us apart."

His chest rises and falls, and it's like a load is lifted off his shoulders. "Thank fuck."

I don't know what's running through his head, but after this, I'm more determined for us to get some counselling. My man is hard as nails, but a man can only take so many knocks, and Winter has taken more than his fair share. We've each been engrossed in our own pain the last few months; it's time we shared it again and getting counselling will hopefully help us do that.

6

Lily

 stare at the bon bons scattered in torn pieces on the kitchen floor and have to work hard to stifle the scream lodged in my chest. It's 10:00 a.m. and I have a club full of families arriving in two hours for our Christmas barbecue, and now I have no fucking Christmas bon bons. On top of that, we still have no air conditioning. King can't fix it, and because it's Christmas Day, he can't find anyone who can. Also, Travis is still not completely well again, and he's been far more needy than usual this morning. I told King it's because of the heat in an effort to force him to find me a miracle cure for the air conditioning. That went down as well as can be expected, i.e. he lost his shit at me. I know I'm being a bitch today, but I. Don't. Care. It's fucking hot and no woman should be expected to run Christmas in this kind of heat.

"Mum, Meredith is hogging the Xbox. She won't let me and Travis have a go," Cade says from behind me.

I spin to face him. I knew this Xbox was going to be the bane of my existence, but King told me it would be their favourite Christmas present. It might be, but it isn't mine. "Where's your father?"

He shrugs. "I don't know."

"You go find him and ask him to help you sort this out. I've got a mess of bon bons to sort out." My temperature is rising and it's not just from the lack of cold air.

Cade scowls but turns to do as I said.

"Cade," I call out as he walks away. "Any idea who did this to the bon bons?"

"Travis," he calls back.

Taking a deep breath, I remind myself it's a crime to kill your own children.

I must not go to jail.

I must not go to jail.

I must not go to jail.

"Lily, darling," my mother says as she glides into the kitchen, twirling in her new skirt. "Brynn just called and she can't drop off the salads she promised to bring over."

I stare at her, willing her to take those words back. "Why not?" We've had this planned for weeks. *Weeks.* On their way to Jamie's parents for lunch, they were going to drop off five huge salads. Salads I need to help me feed all the people coming today.

Mum looks at me like I'm a crazy person. "They're having car trouble. She said you'd be better off getting someone to collect them." Frowning, she adds, "Is everything okay, darling?"

If I still smoked, I'd smoke an entire packet right now.

"Take a look at the kitchen floor, Mum. Does everything look okay? Do you feel okay in this hot-as-fuck house? Can you even hear yourself with all the noise the kids are making?"

The sound of boots thudding on the floor causes me to turn, coming face to face with King. He directs his attention to Mum and says, "Hannah, can you give us a minute?"

"I think it might be a good idea," Mum murmurs before leaving us alone.

King's eyes come back to me. "What's going on?"

I gesture at the floor. "Look at what your son did to the bon bons."

He takes a look but doesn't seem as perturbed as I am.

I don't give him the chance to say anything before saying, "That's all the bon bons, King. All of them! I have zero spares."

"For fuck's sake, Lily, they're just bon bons. Who did it?"

My eyes almost explode from my face. "At this point, I don't really care who did it; I just care that we now have no bon bons for lunch."

"We don't need them."

"Yes, we do!"

"No one will care if we don't have them."

"I'll care." I throw my hands in the air and stalk away from him to the pantry. This conversation is not helpful.

"Lily!" he barks. "Don't walk away from me."

I carry on. "I've got things to do for your lunch. I don't have time for this conversation."

He catches up to me and grabs me by the waist. Spinning me to face him, he demands, "*My* lunch? I wasn't the one who fucking wanted this lunch."

I place my hands to his chest trying to push him away, but he's got a tight hold on me. "No, but I'm doing it for you. For your club."

His eyes flash with frustration as he backs me against the wall. "What's really going on here?"

"The only thing going on here is that the bon bons are ruined, the air con is broken, the kids are feral, and my husband's slowing me down by—"

"Bullshit. You've been on edge all morning. Why are you so fucking worked up about some bon bons?"

"Because I wanted this lunch to be perfect for you and the club. That's fucking why! You've all had a shit year and things only seem to be getting worse. Your guys are all stressed. Their families are all stressed. You're never home. The kids are missing you. I'm missing you. We all need some happy in our lives and I wanted to give it to everyone today. And Christmas needs bon bons!"

I'm hot.

I'm bothered.

And I'm done.

I push him away and make a move to get as far from this kitchen as possible. But King snakes his arm around my waist and pulls me back to him.

"I fucking love you, woman," he growls. "But you need to let me do the worrying over my club. This isn't shit I want you stressing over."

"But I do worry over it. I've always worried about you and your guys. I hate seeing you all go through so much. Bringing some happy into your lives is something little I can do for you all."

He brings his hand to my cheek and cups it, gently rubbing his thumb over my lips. "Bringing happy is good, but not if it costs you. I don't like seeing you this stressed. I fucking *won't* see you this stressed." He pauses for a moment, thinking. "I'll get more bon bons. Is there anything else on your list of shit-causing-you-hell? Besides the fucking air con, that is. You've already busted my balls over that and I'm still trying, but it's not looking good."

The mention of the air con makes me smile.

King caring makes me smile.

And just like that, I feel like I can breathe again.

"I need someone to go over to Brynn's and collect some salads."

"Consider it handled. Anything else?"

I press my body into his. "You know, you're not a bad husband after all. I think I'll keep you."

"Who the fuck said anything about me being a bad husband?"

I arch my brows. "Well, there *are* times where you can be a pain in my ass. But like I said, I'll keep you around a bit longer."

"You just try and get rid of me. It's never fucking happening."

I loop my hands around his neck. "Promise me you'll fuck me tonight. I'm dying over here."

"You and me fucking both," he mutters. Then, pulling away from me, he says, "I need to get out of here before I fuck you against this wall. I'll take care of the bon bons and get the salads from Brynn. I want you in the bath calming the fuck down while

I'm gone. And when I get back, maybe I'll have sorted out the air con, too."

"I can't just take a bath, King. Someone needs to watch these kids of yours."

"I'll ask your mother to do it. You need some time out."

God, a bath sounds like heaven. I can't recall the last time I had one. It used to be a nightly ritual for me, but with all the chaos and exhaustion of the last few months, I've taken to collapsing into bed at the end of every day without even thinking of the bath.

He wraps his hand around my neck and pulls me close again so he can kiss me. "Fuck knows, I want you wired for my dick today, and at the moment, I'm half convinced you're wired for my blood instead. Take a bath."

With that, he exits the kitchen and I'm left thinking about his goddam dick. The man needs to know I think about it far more often than is productive.

I reach for my phone and send him a text.

ME: Just FYI, your dick is wired into my brain. I wake up thinking about it. I spend far too long thinking about it every day. And I think about it at night when I make myself come. I don't need to take a bath to get me ready for it.

. . .

HIS TEXT COMES through a few minutes later.

KING: Fucking hell, Lily. I'm hard as fuck here. Don't send me shit like that when I have shit to do for you.

Me: Good. That makes two of us. You better work your magic tonight and make sure none of our kids are sick. If there's no dick tonight, there will be hell to pay.

King: Get in the fucking bath.

Me: I love you too xx

7

Zara

*M*e: Is your air conditioning still not working?

Mum: I'm in the bath and feeling all relaxed and now you've gone and ruined it.

Me: Why are you in the bath?

Mum: King ordered me into it.

Me: Oh God.

I CALL HER. God knows what's going on over there.

"I've got at least another fifteen minutes in here,

Zara. Can we not discuss the state of my air conditioning? I'm trying to stay Zen-like."

"Zen-like? You wouldn't know how to be Zen-like if you tried."

"A girl can pretend."

"Yes, any girl but my mother. It's the Christmas Crazies, isn't it? That's why he's put you in the bath."

"It's because of the bon bons that he put me in the bath."

"Okay, now you're sounding like a true crazy person, Mum. What in the heck is going on over there?"

She tells me what happened and then says, "As for the air con, it's still not working. King is still trying to get it fixed, but I've accepted my fate and fully expect to be sweating my ass off for days."

"Right, so I should dress appropriately. Good to know. That's all I was texting for. You may return to your Zen mission."

We end the call and I choose a dress to wear to the barbecue. I then pull my hair up into a messy bun to keep it off my shoulders.

Fury has taken Noah to his mother's house and should be home soon. The three of us had a great time this morning opening presents and having Christmas breakfast together. And celebrating my birthday. They spoiled me with yummy food and lots of love; I haven't felt this special on my birthday since I was a kid and Mum spoiled me.

As I head into the laundry to set a load of washing to wash this afternoon, a text comes through.

KING: You got any bon bons at your place?

Me: I have three spare ones.

King: Bring them with you today.

Me: You having trouble finding enough?

King: Yeah.

Me: Well at least Mum is all Zen-like in her bath. Good job. She's been crazy for days.

HE DOESN'T SEND any more texts; I figure he's got a mission and a half ahead of him trying to source bon bons on Christmas Day. I can't wait to find out if he pulls it off, but then again, this is King; the man can pull miracles out of his ass when it comes to making Mum happy.

I'm drawn from my thoughts when I hear the garage door open and Fury's ute drive in. My belly does flips at the thought of being alone with him.

I hurry out to the garage but come to a stop just outside it when I hear the sound of a dog and then

Fury saying, "Shh, you're supposed to be a surprise, little one."

My heart melts at what he says.

The last time he was home, we hung out with some of my work friends at a picnic in a park and one of them had a dog with them. The dog took to Fury, and I loved watching him play with it. Later that night, as we were falling asleep, I'd told him how much I'd love a dog. The man never forgets anything I tell him.

The door to the garage opens and Fury comes into view. He's holding the cutest little white French bulldog in his arms and I melt some more. Watching Fury with his son is an ovary explosion in the making; I'm pretty sure watching him with this dog is going to be the same.

His face breaks out in a smile before he looks down at the puppy and says, "This is your mummy." And then, looking back up at me, he says, "Merry Christmas, baby," before handing the dog to me.

I take the puppy from him, surprised and excited all in one. "You bought me a dog?"

He moves closer so he can kiss me. "Well, she's both of ours so long as you don't decide to stop test driving me. And if you do, then she's all yours. But since we both know I'm never letting you go, you have to share her with me."

"Oh my God! We have a dog!" I bend my face so I

can kiss her, and she gets all excited, licking me and wiggling in my arms. When I've got my fill of her, I pull Fury in for another kiss. "Thank you! This really is the best birthday and Christmas ever."

"You take her inside. I've just gotta get her food and toys out of the car. And you need to think of a name for her."

I smile, already knowing her name.

When I don't say anything, he prods me, "You already have one, don't you?"

My smile grows. "Grace."

Ever since the time four years ago when he told me to give myself some grace, I've never forgotten his advice and have often repeated it to myself in times of need. And sometimes we say it to each other now. It's definitely one of our things, and the name is perfect for our first baby together.

"I like it." I don't miss the emotion in his voice and that only stirs mine more.

"Thank you for making today so special for me," I say softly.

"The first of many, princess." He jerks his chin. "Take her inside and show her around. I'll be in in a minute."

In a gush of excited energy, I plant one more kiss on his lips and then take my baby inside. Placing her on the floor, I say, "Okay, Gracie, no peeing inside, okay? It's my only rule. Well, that and don't eat my plants. Oh, and don't chew things that aren't your toys, especially not my clothes." I pause for a moment. "I guess I have more than one rule, huh?"

While I'm babbling to her, she's sniffing everything in sight and then takes off down the hallway. I struggle to keep up with her as she runs through the house exploring, and when Fury finds us, we're in our bedroom.

His deep chuckle comes from the doorway as I'm bending over, trying to coax Grace out from under the bed. "If getting a dog means your ass is gonna be in the air multiple times a day, I've just made the best decision of my life."

I straighten and meet his gaze. "I thought having Noah and then making me your woman were the best decisions of your life."

He walks my way as Grace runs between us. Grabbing a handful of my dress, he pulls me to him. "I take it back. They were. This is just the best decision of today."

"No, the best decision of today will be when you decide to take my dress off."

He lifts my dress; however, I stop him and add, "But first we need to get Gracie set up."

"Fuck," he mutters with a shake of his head. "She's gonna come before me now, isn't she?"

"Well, babies always come first. Even furbabies."

He lets my dress go. "Always keeping me on my

toes" is all I hear him say as he scoops Grace up and carries her out of the bedroom.

I'm the luckiest girl in the world, that's for damn sure. And this is just the beginning of our life together.

8

Birdie

"Here's the bon bons King asked for," I say to Lily, handing over the pack of ten that Mum sacrificed for King. "Did he manage to find enough?"

"I don't know, and to be honest, I've moved on from worrying over them," she says as she takes a sip of wine. "He came home, told me to have a drink, and to sit back and relax because he's taking over the barbecue. So that's what I'm doing."

"Good man." I motion at her glass. "You need to pour me one too. God knows I could do with it."

Her brows pull together. "Why? What's happened?"

"You know how we were talking about Winter and me maybe needing to see a counsellor?" At her nod, I continue. "I think the time has come. And it freaks me out a little. Digging into our shit."

She squeezes my hand. "Yeah, I know it does. But there's a lot of stuff you two need to talk about."

I swallow down the fear clawing at me. "What if it's stuff we shouldn't talk about? What if it rips open too many wounds we can't recover from?" I'll never leave Winter again and I know he's a loyal-to-the-end man; my greatest worry is we become disconnected and live our marriage as two lonely people.

"Birdie, not talking about it may cause those wounds to fester to the point that nothing can heal them. There's that possibility too, and you need to consider that."

She's right. I know she is, and I've already made up my mind to convince Winter of counselling, but still, this fear never leaves my side these days.

Zara joins us before I can agree with Lily, and greets her mother with a kiss. "Holy shit, these fans are bomb. Did King get them?" she asks as she surveys the backyard of King and Lily's place where huge industrial fans are scattered around.

"Yes," Lily says. "I don't know where from and I don't care. I'm just happy I'm sitting in front of one.

And I'm also happy that the kids are playing with the other children, not a fight in sight. I know I'm gonna have to get up and do some work at some point, but for now, I'm getting my wine on."

"Lil," Tatum calls out from under the marquee near us that's set up with the food. "Are the salads in the fridge upstairs or downstairs?"

"Upstairs," Lily says, making a move to get up.

I slow her. "I'll go. You keep getting your wine on."

"This is why I love you, B," she says. "By the time you get back, I'll have one ready for you."

I don't get to see Lily often these days, but when I do, it's like we were never apart. We came into the Storm world around the same time and helped each other find our footing. And being married to club presidents means we share many similarities in what we're dealing with club wise. It's at times like this, when we get the chance to catch up and talk about our struggles that I'm reminded of how blessed I am to have her in my life.

Leaving her with Zara, I head upstairs for the salads. I'm surprised when I find Winter exiting the kitchen.

"Hey, you," I greet him. "Good timing. Can you help me carry some salads downstairs?"

An easy smile fills his face and he takes hold of

my waist. Pulling me inside, he says, "Only if you do something for me."

That smile of his, along with the sexy hum of his voice and the way his hands are all over me, stirs a wave of flutters in my tummy. "That depends on what it is you want. I mean, there's no way I'm dropping to my knees and sucking your dick right now, but I'm open to other options."

"Angel," he says with a grin, "I would never ask you to do that. I'd at least find us a room if I wanted my dick sucked."

I move into him, loving when he banters with me like this. It used to be our way, but everything we've gone through has slowly taken that from us. Every now and then we find our way back, but it never lasts long. Life can be a cruel bitch sometimes; I want to look her dead in the eyes and punch her out. But for now, I'll take every minute with Winter like this that I can get.

"Okay," I say. "Tell me what you want me to do, sexy man, and I'll see if it's a possibility."

"Sexy man," he rumbles, heat gathering in his eyes. "I like that. You should call me that more often."

Goodness. My tummy is flip-flopping all over the place now. *Give me more.* "We're running out of time here. Are you gonna tell me?"

His easy mood shifts into a more serious one. "I want you to get out of here with me."

Not what I was expecting. Not at all. "As in, you want to leave already?"

"As in I want to spend the day alone with you. We could take a drive to the beach. Maybe go swimming. Eat ice creams. Talk. Just you and me. Like we used to before life got so fucked up."

Every inch of my skin buzzes with excitement and happiness at what he's just suggested. "I would love that."

He takes that in and nods slowly. "Yeah, me too. Show me where the salads are and I'll take them down while you go and tell Lily we're leaving. I know you two were looking forward to catching up."

I reach for his neck and bring his face to mine. "I love you, sexy man." I kiss him and don't miss the smile on his lips. I can also feel how some of the tightness in his body has disappeared. I don't know what's caused that, but I'm all for it.

"You keep this sexy-man business up," he says, "and fuck knows how many orgasms you'll get tonight."

"What, you mean I won't get any this afternoon?"

With a shake of his head, he says, "No. This afternoon isn't about sex, Birdie. While I won't be able to keep my hands off you, I want us to spend some time doing the things we don't do enough of these days."

I just fell in love with my husband all over again.

Maybe there is light at the end of this dark tunnel we've been in for years. I've always believed that to be true, but after our greatest loss three months ago, I've started to doubt it. Now, my heart is hopeful again.

9

Lily

"The kids are out," King says, joining me in our bedroom just after 9:00 p.m. "How are you feeling?"

I smile, feeling every ounce of it in my entire body. After a rocky start to the day, it's been a good Christmas. King came through with everything—well, except for the air conditioning, but I've moved past that—and he went out of his way to help me make the barbecue a good time for his guys. "I'm feeling happy."

He brings his hand to my throat, wrapping his

fingers around it. "Good," he says, his voice filled with gravel. "Are you tired?"

I know what he's asking and the answer is no.

I shake my head.

He bends his face to mine and kisses me.

He's rough.

It's a promise of what's to come.

And I'm weak at the knees for more.

But just when I think I know what's next, he surprises me by ending the kiss and letting me go. "I've spoken to Winter and I won't be staying in Melbourne once we've taken care of the thing we've got on this week."

My brain is slow to catch up to what he's saying. "What? You're coming home straight away?"

"Yeah. I'll leave tomorrow and I should be back home in a week or so."

"And then you're what? Staying here?"

He nods. "You need me here."

I put my hands up between us. "No, King. I won't come between you and what you need to do for the club. I'm good now. I can—"

"You're not good, Lily. And neither are the kids. They need me here as much as you do."

I shake my head repeatedly. "This isn't what I want. Not if it's not what the club needs. I just wanted you home for longer than a few days, that's all."

"This is what's happening." His statement is forceful. It's his way of saying "end of story," but as far as I'm concerned, it's not the end of anything. We need to discuss this some more.

"Okay, so you do this. How long will it be before you resent the fact you're home when your club needs you?"

"They won't need me in Melbourne after this."

"You don't know that for sure."

He scrubs a hand over his face, his eyes glinting with frustration. King's not a fan of defending his decisions, but sometimes I challenge him regardless. "Fucking hell, Lily, I thought you'd be happy about this."

"If it's what you actually want, then I'm all for it. But if you're only doing it because you think it'll make me happy, I'm out. We should come to a better compromise. One that works for both of us."

He turns silent. Contemplative. And then, moving faster than I see coming, he takes hold of my throat again and rasps, "This *is* what I want. Fuck"—his voice is strangled with the level of emotion I rarely see in my husband—"it's what I need. I need to be home with you and the kids. Don't fucking fight me on it."

His words, and what I hear from him and see in him, all combine deep inside me, and I'm unable to hold myself back. I'm overcome with emotion that his admission brings out in me.

I love everything about King, even his moods and bossy ways, but *this* is one of my favourite parts of him: his raw honesty.

Grasping his face, I say, "God, I love you."

With that, he finally gives in to our need for each other. Keeping one hand around my neck, he kisses me roughly again while undoing the tie of my dress. Once he has it undone, he pulls his lips from mine and strips me of my dress.

His eyes roam my body, hungry and filled with dark desires.

I'd do anything to grant him those desires.

"Fuck, you're beautiful," he growls right before he lifts me and carries me to our bed.

In a few quick moves, he has me on the mattress and his clothes off.

Positioning himself on top of me, he says, "This is gonna be fast. Hold the fuck on," right before he thrusts inside me.

I wrap every limb around him and hold the fuck on as he shows me exactly what he meant last night when he said he wanted to slam his dick so hard inside me it'd break me.

He doesn't break me. But fuck me, he does a good job trying.

And I love every minute of it.

He's right: it is fast. We come together, the pleasure so intense I lose myself until King pulls out of me.

Kneeling, he runs his hand over the bare skin of my stomach, his eyes glued to my pussy. I know from experience that he's already worked out how he wants to fuck me tonight. And that he'll take his time with me now.

Bringing his eyes to mine, he says, "I haven't given you your Christmas present yet."

"We said no presents for each other this year."

He ignores me and moves off the bed, disappearing into the walk-in robe. A few moments later, he reappears and comes back to me, a jewellery box in his hand. The blue box he knows I love.

"Shit, King, I didn't get you anything. I thought we agreed to put the money towards—"

"We did, and I don't want anything, but there's no fucking way I'm not getting you something."

I open the box and almost squeal with delight when I see the beautiful silver Tiffany bow bracelet inside. "Oh my God, I love it!" With the box still in my hand, I scramble so I can climb into his lap. Kissing him with every bit of love and happiness I'm feeling, I then say, "And I love *you*. Not because of this bracelet, though, but because I know you would go to hell and back to give our family and me what we need. Thank you for loving us so well."

His arms come around me. Tightly, like he's keeping me close, protecting me from something. But then that's King, always protecting me. "I never liked Christmas until you came into my life." He stops talking abruptly and I know that whatever he has to say is going to be big for him.

"I know," I say softly, running my fingers through his hair.

"Still then, it took me a few years to let those old feelings go. Now, I look forward to it, your crazy shit and all. The kids, the toys, the arguments, the food, all of it." He squeezes me tighter. "You gave that to me, Lily, and every fucking day you give me your love and care. I'll fucking do anything to keep you happy because you've made me the happiest fucking man alive."

My heart fills with love for the man in front of me, and I'm almost certain I'm going to cry, but for now, I manage to keep my shit together. "For an asshole, you sometimes say the nicest things to me."

He lifts me and forces me onto my back. "Put the bracelet on," he growls. "And stop talking. The only thing I wanna hear while I taste your cunt is your screams of pleasure."

I might love King's infrequent declarations of love, but what I need even more than that is him like this. Filthy, demanding, and unapologetically untamed.

Merry freaking Christmas to me.

Thank you so much for reading Christmas Hearts!! I hope you loved it as much as I loved writing it. Being back with my Storm couples is a happy place for me.

WANNA READ A BONUS SCENE featuring Fury & Zara? I mean, he promised her a "rain check and then some" and we never got to read that in this story! Sign up here for it: http://ninalevinebooks.com/join

NEXT BOOK IN THE SERIES

BATTLE HEARTS
COMING JANUARY 28, 2020

Love, fight, battle, protect: the Morrison way.
The only fucking way.

This is Winter's journey to MC president.
This is Winter & Birdie's journey to building a family.
This is one epic MC battle.

The conclusion to everything started in War of Hearts.

PREORDER BATTLE HEARTS - https://
ninalevinebooks.com/storm-mc-reloaded#battle-
hearts

WANT MORE OF MY STORM MEN? I love writing
bonus scenes and share them in my Alpha Vault
which all my email subscribers have access to. If
you'd love access, join here: http://
ninalevinebooks.com/join

If you're on Facebook, I have a reader group you can
join to chat about my books with me, enter exclusive
giveaways and read sneak peeks of upcoming books.
Join here: https://www.facebook.com/
groups/LevinesLadies/

If you loved this book, please consider leaving a
review for it on your favourite book site. I appreciate
you helping spread the word about my books by
reviewing and telling friends about them!

Follow me on BookBub to hear about my sales:
https://www.bookbub.com/authors/nina-levine

ALSO BY NINA LEVINE

Storm MC Series

Sydney Storm MC Series

Storm MC Reloaded Series

Hurricane Hearts (#1)

War of Hearts (#2)

Christmas Hearts (#3)

Battle Hearts (#4)

The Hardy Family Series

Steal My Breath (single dad romance)

Crave Series

Be The One (rockstar romance)

Billionaire Romance

Ashton Scott

www.ninalevinebooks.com

ABOUT THE AUTHOR

Nina Levine

Dreamer.

Coffee Lover.

Gypsy at heart.

USA Today bestselling author who writes about alpha men & the women they love.

When I'm not creating with words you will find me planning my next getaway, visiting somewhere new in the world, having a long conversation over coffee and cake with a friend, creating with paper or curled up with a good book and chocolate.

I've been writing since I was twelve. Weaving words together has always been a form of therapy for me especially during my harder times. These days I'm proud that my words help others just as much as they help me.

www.ninalevinebooks.com

Cover Design by Romantic Book Affair Designs

Editing by Becky Johnson, Hot Tree Editing

Made in the USA
Coppell, TX
19 February 2021

50500006R00062